T0298281

THE GREAT AMERICAN DISASTER

THE FRENCH LIST

Shmuel T. Meyer

THE GREAT AMERICAN DISASTER

SHORT STORIES

Followed by

A LUNCH OF LIGHT

TRANSLATED BY
GILA WALKER

LONDON NEW YORK CALCUTTA

This volume is part of a boxed set
titled *And the War Is Over* . . .
Not to be sold separately.

Seagull Books, 2024

Originally published in French as *The Great American Disaster*
© 2021 Les Éditions Metropolis, Geneva

English translation © Gila Walker, 2024

First published in English translation by Seagull Books, 2024

ISBN 978 1 8030 9 340 6

British Library Cataloguing-in-Publication Data
A catalogue record for this book is available from the British Library

Typeset by Seagull Books, Calcutta, India
Printed and bound by Hyam Enterprises, Calcutta, India

As life runs on, the road grows strange
With faces new and near the end
The milestones into headstones change,
'Neath every one a friend.

James Russel Lowell

to Chantal M.P., Michèle S., Chiara C., Nicole G.,
Lully D. and Liliane L.K.,
François K., Benoît M. and Asher B.

CONTENTS

NEW YORK STEAM COMPANY

"I've never understood why certain bodies float so well."

Lieutenant Gantz, hunched over like a bent nail, lit his cigarette, blocking the wind with the turned-up collar of his pitch-black thick wool coat. He puffed out the smoke in small clouds that blew right back at his face. It was the kind of cold that extinguishes any sense of vanity, a blistering fucking frost that nips every tissue in your body and dislocates your bones.

The naval sergeant retrieving the body with a gaff was a young, already pot-bellied fellow, flushed as much from his efforts as from the cold and an onset of rosacea. Lieutenant Driscoll, Gantz's partner, muttered between his rotting teeth, "Never understood why certain bodies float so well." And, in this case, he was right on the button. The girl that the guy leaning over the rail of his tub boat was hauling in on the tip of his gaff floated magnificently well. Her long auburn head of hair was like the corolla of a very delicate and transparent oval face. Her outstretched arms

1

made her look like she was swimming in the pool of some Florida resort. Her flowery skirt mocked the calendar, bringing a bright touch of blue to the expansive gray canvas of the East River. She floated there, trapped under one of the piers of the Queensboro Bridge, the one close to East 59th Street and the yellow-brick smokestack of the New York Steam Company.

The corpse, once on the pavement, dripped, forming a dark puddle, the liquid shadow of dead catfish. Kovalchuk, the coroner, was drafting a preliminary report on the hood of a shiny red Star Chief. He hadn't bothered to take off his gloves. The tip of his chewed pencil jiggled between his fingers. He grumbled about the cold, about stupid bitches who floated in the East River on a fucking Sunday in January, about the shitty quality of New York State government paper. He hurled insults at Governor Rockefeller and cursed his descendants for a hundred generations. She had water in her lungs, an aquarium-full with no goldfish. She was no more than twenty-four and had a pair of tits . . .

The McGill Brothers bar, two blocks from East 67th, was the cops' backroom, their refuge, their hangout between the precinct and their beds. Gantz downed two double Bulleits drowned in seltzer water, watched the bubbles move down the sides of the glass while chewing on a three-tier tuna-cucumber sandwich with enough mayonnaise to cement the entire Pan Am Building going up over Grand Central Station.

Outside, the street was hazy, dense with scents rising from the river, a nauseating mix of silt and sulfur, putrid seaweed, and factory smoke. Saul Gantz knew all the smells of the city; the old ones, decaying vegetables, silvery carps, stale pretzels, and rye bread in the Rutgers Street market; the new ones, curry and industrial pizzas; and the everlasting smell of burned Bakelite and steaming asphalt on Broadway after a summer rain. He claimed he could tell from the smell whether he was on the banks of the Hudson or the East River. He was probably bragging when he said he could find his way blindfolded from East to West and from North to South.

Ray Kovaltchuk, a fat buttock pressing down on Gantz' desk, recited his litany like a Ukrainian widow her rosary: Tal Hammerstein, twenty-seven, Newark, New Jersey, reported missing on December 26, a beatnik on drugs, a damn kike with a hell of a pair of tits . . .

*

In the ten years since the Pusan Perimeter and his return from Korea, seven since the Police Academy, and three since his transfer from Queens to the Upper East Side precinct on 67th Street, he'd seen so many dead bodies, so many chunks of meat, that they'd peeled away, one by one, like onion skins, any convictions he might have had about the promises of humanity and messianic days to come. He'd hit the booze, like all the others, dabbled in chemicals, but nothing helped. Every day Saul Gantz lost a layer of skin that made him fragile, more vaporous than a ghost.

*

Sunday was succumbing to the hideous milky light of the neons. The three detectives on duty were leafing through the latest issue of *Playboy* spouting obscenities that rose in intensity as they turned the pages.

Doc Johnson, the coroner, was in Atlantic City, celebrating his third marriage in five years. His obsession was with strippers, go-go dancers, and showgirls at Lady J and Ginger Cat, preferably with red hair and C-cups. So, because of Atlantic City, nipple tassels, and redheads on the podium, the autopsy wasn't scheduled until the following day and Tal Hammerstein would have to spend a night in the fridge before being ripped open, gutted, and sewn back up by the libidinous butcher from the OCME, the medical examiner's office.

*

At 7 p.m., the mother had identified her daughter on the stainless steel table, her body intact and white, frozen under the green sheet, her lips and eyelids swollen.

Gantz put out an orange filter burning in the ashtray with the rest of the cold coffee in his cup. On the stairs, he crossed paths with Driscoll, told him he was going home, and noticed that his partner reeked of alcohol and grease.

A dreary drizzle was playing with the street lights. Dignified old Jews were leaving Park East Synagogue, waving goodbye to the rabbi. Gantz could have stopped and exchanged a word or two with him. Told him that a little Tal Hammerstein from Newark was dead. But the rabbi was definitely too young, possibly too clean-shaven, to be of any consolation. So he walked quickly, stopped out of breath under an awning to light a cigarette. He turned south on Third Avenue, then headed east on 59th to the smokestack of the New York Steam Company. At the railing overlooking the river, he tossed the butt of his last cigarette with a flick of the wrist, then murmured the opening words of kaddish, thinking it would be a long time before a body would float so well.

"IT NEVER ENTERED MY MIND"

To photographer Herman Leonard

Abbey had landed there thanks to Max Roach and me thanks to *DownBeat* magazine. She sang and I freelanced at $6.25 a page. She wanted to be a great jazz singer; I'd given myself three years before winning the Pulitzer. To make the story short, Abbey was as sweet as a candy cane that Charlie Parker's drummer dreamed of licking and I was a hungry milksop from the Weequahic neighborhood of Newark, New Jersey.

My father's Mercury was rumbling on Interstate 78 and I was pissed it wasn't a convertible. It was an incredibly beautiful afternoon in May. The sun was building a small fortune of reflections as I crossed Hackensack River. Straight ahead, facing me, the smokestacks of the Croxton and Jersey City factories were puffing out elegantly billowing columns of white smoke. The trees in Ridgefield Park seemed to have been colored by a child intent on using all the green shades from his box of Conncolor colored pencils.

They were all there already, inside their glass cage. Rudy Van Gelder was supervising the recording, playing with balances and volumes. For eight hours he and Thelma, his assistant, had been watching with fascination the "five tranquil guys in a state of grace" (those were Thelma's words and the title of my article) inventing the most beautiful music that I'd be given to hear for the next fifty years.

After having been pissed about the convertible not being one, I was now pissed that I'd missed eight hours of recording without knowing that I was embarking for the next nine. Off on the side, five of us were squeezed together on the battered gray-velvet bench seat: Frances Taylor, Bob Weinstock, Max Roach, Abbey Lincoln, and me.

At the time I'd already adopted the technique that would always stick to me of jotting down everything I observed in a small spiral notebook. From the most insignificant to the most significant. It could be the patterns created by condensation on the window, Rudy undoing his bow tie, Miles wiping the spittle from his trumpet, the ash from the cigarette hanging from Red Garland's mouth, the sweat stains around Philly Joe Jones's armpits, the silver signet on Paul Chambers's ring finger climbing up and down the neck of his double bass like an insect, Thelma's elaborate hairdo collapsing after having probably emptied a whole can of hairspray to ensure eight hours of provincial distinction, Abbey's marvelous legs, Frances's yellow high heels, Bob Weinstock's childlike glee, and the wild yet veiled look in John Coltrane's eyes.

When I arrived, the quintet was just finishing the second take of "Surrey with the Fringe on Top," a sax cover by Coltrane framed by two minutes forty-two seconds of delicate muted trumpet and Red Garland's sunny solo.

At around five in the afternoon, we took the first group pause on the steps of the stairway to the Van Gelder studios. Miles handed out smokes from his crumpled pack of Luckies to no one in particular. Max Roach dashed out to make it to the Apollo before rush hour. I made the most of the opportunity to glean a few words here and there, satisfied grunts from Chambers, snatches of jokes from Garland, a learned exegesis from Miles Davis. In the bathroom, I saw Coltrane snorting a line on the edge of the sink.

To my surprise, Abbey hadn't followed Max Roach to Manhattan. She was talking with Frances and Miles and I didn't dare intrude on their conversation. After the perfect beauty of her face, the curve of her legs, and the incredible finesse of her naked arms, I'd finally heard her voice and you can believe me when I say that it in no way altered the instinctive (quasi-animal) fascination that I had for her.

I was twenty-five, a nice smile that cost my mother a pretty penny to buy from Dr. Goresky of Hoboken, and a French aftershave that served, primo, to make others think that I'd shaved although I didn't need to and, secundo, to distract from my shabby suburban clothes.

After the break, Miles asked everyone to pick up with "It Never Entered My Mind." No score, just the inconceivable elegance of the horn and Red Garland who fancied he was Chopin.

Honestly, I couldn't have agreed more with Baudelaire—who was French, like my aftershave—when he wrote of beauty, "that renders the hero cowardly and the infant courageous." Ah, to take Abbey's lips and swear to be faithful to my dying day. Instead of that, I shot her a stupid Weequahic grin, an all-too-Goresky grimace that I regretted as soon as the dimples of my hairless cheeks symmetrically approached my ears and I observed my defeat in the eyes of my Dulcinea from Toboso. I could have, more timidly, touched her hand or her knee, tried to capture the fragrances. Instead of that I chose to shut my eyes, abandoning the world, and float on the snare drum swept by Philly Joe Jones's brush. Head tilted backwards on the back of the sofa, I offered my youthful profile to my magnificent neighbor with the double disadvantage of, primo, not knowing whether she was looking at me and, secundo, submitting to her aesthetic judgment my sharply arched nose and my thick lower lip from Weequahic, the Jewish neighborhood of Newark.

Around midnight, the bottles of bourbon appeared. This break was marked by the utter and definitive collapse of Thelma's hairdo and the words pronounced by Miles Davis, henceforth etched for all time on the marble of jazz history: Damn are we good!! To which Bob Weinstock replied, "Pour me another glass, Thelma," which has only remained in my mind and on a scribbled page in my spiral notebook.

In the bathroom where Frances, Red Garland, and I went to smoke a joint of Mary Jane as thick as Count Basie's thumb, "Trane" snorted his umpteenth line on the sink. After the break, they started on "Four." And there, Coltrane, soberly, without swaying, perfectly in line with the big mic marked with the initials VG proved to be the most angelic of the bad boys. He breathed into his instrument like a boxer between each blow to his opponent. He showered the studio with a victor's joy. Abbey winked at me and, no doubt a bit tipsy, she did two or three dance steps. She was barefoot and, without hearing the sound, I could just feel in my groin the swish of her stockings on the carpet.

Then came "Half Nelson" and bop was back in the lead. Miles was hitting the valves and rivalling Dizzy, and Coltrane, vying with Charlie Parker, was doing likewise on the keys of his tenor sax. Under the circumstance, you simply had to move, you couldn't do otherwise, it was as natural as getting up on your feet at a match between Sugar Ray and LaMotta in Madison Square Garden. Frances, who was a dancer and also stoned, kicked her yellow heels across the studio. Miles took advantage of Jones's solo to empty the spittle from his trumpet onto the wine-colored carpet.

I took Abbey's hand and she didn't pull away from my embrace. The spiral notebook fell from my pocket and all the words packed between its pages.

At three in the morning, the session ended on the steps of the stairway to the Van Gelder studio.

The disheveled Thelma who lived in Englewood on the other side of the river left with her boss and Bob Weinstock in a white Dodge. Miles, Frances, and Coltrane took a taxi back to Manhattan. Chambers and Jones, who knew a bar that was still open in Hackensack, didn't insist that we come with them.

I took Abbey back to her place on Grand Concourse. I railed about the damned Mercury that was still not a convertible. Driving over the Washington Bridge, with all the lights of New York City flashing in the Hudson, Abbey laid her lovely frizzy head on my shoulder and tucked under her magnificent legs clad in silk.

THE PUSAN PERIMETER

Saul Gantz hasn't a clue how to iron. He's going to have to do it anyway since Rosalinda hasn't come for over two weeks and he's got nothing left to put on his back or his butt. Today it's not a matter of elegance but of hygiene.

The smell of the iron's hot soleplate and the starch have brought back memories of his childhood, his mother, and the shabby two-room apartment on Penn Street. All in all, he didn't do such a bad job. He had a hard time with the sleeves, with the buttons too, which kept getting caught. Looking attentively at his clothes made him realize that they weren't in great shape, collars and cuffs frayed, worn-out pants bottoms, unstitched hems. Something like his life, like his apartment on Eckford Street. Not really dirty, not really clean either. An apartment, a transient existence.

When God decides for his pleasure to complicate your life, he doesn't restrain himself. As soon as Lieutenant Gantz arrived at the 67th Street precinct, he bumped right into Ray Kovaltchuk walking with a mug of coffee in his hand. Gantz's shirt and tie were now adorned with a nice brown stain, which only his jacket could hide. The worst was that the stain would not even arouse anyone's attention. To all his colleagues the lieutenant was a nice guy, to be sure, competent, no doubt, incorruptible, for certain, but he smacked of trouble and bad luck. All in all, he was a schlimazel, a subscriber to the wrong number in life.

Tal Hammerstein, the girl found at the Queensboro Bridge, was a closed suicide case. That was last winter. No one in the precinct remembered her or the terrible cold that hit New York that month of January. They had finally received the budget to install air-conditioning and the officers had only one thing on their minds: avoiding going out into the scorching August heat. Mayor Wagner had, to his credit, the construction of the Pan Am Building and, to his discredit, that of Lincoln Center, but he was also held responsible for an uptick in violence in the poor neighborhoods of the city. The heat made things worse. Not a day went by without a murder occurring, not only in Harlem but also in the Lower East Side or the Bronx. There were shootings on Amsterdam Avenue, in Times Square, and even on the Upper West Side. Scores were being settled between gangs, between junkies, between pimps and hookers, between pimps and pimps. So, Tal Hammerstein's floating body . . .

And yet the kid had not left Saul's mind for an instant. Both the girl and the mother. For months it was all a tangle in his foggy head. When he thought of the daughter, he saw the mother's face. He saw her walking toward him down the white-tiled corridor in the morgue, clutching the flaps of her threadbare wool coat to her chest, ignoring the lock of hair slipping over her forehead and the wing of her nose. The clacking of her high heels on the tiles. The run in the stocking on her left leg. The all-too-heady scent of her perfume when he gripped her elbow, as much to keep her from collapsing as to force her to leave the room that reeked of formaldehyde and chlorine.

So, Tal's floating body . . . Lieutenant Gantz hadn't forgotten it when Thelma Hammerstein showed up in the 67th Street precinct. She looked frailer than she had in winter. A skimpy, knee-length dress with blue flowers, white gloves and a navy-blue purse. Kovaltchuk pointed with his thumb to the lieutenant's glass cubicle and Gantz adjusted his stained tie over his stained shirt. As he stood up, he tightened the belt of his pants, combed his outspread fingers through his hair.

Thelma had come to get a death certificate for Essex County and wanted to thank him for his kindness at the time of the tragedy. She pronounced the word tragedy with eyes downcast and head lowered. The lock had slipped out of her elaborate hairdo again and was flapping against the wing of her freckled nose. They went out for a drink. Gantz considered for a moment taking her to McGill's, but then he decided it would be better to go someplace less frequented by the precinct cops. Not being suitably dressed for the bar they chose on Lexington Avenue, they played it up, exaggerating their chutzpah as Jewish escapees from the Lower East Side.

Then he'd stopped by his place to change and had met up with Thelma in the Village. Cal Tjader was playing with Horne, Schreiber, Discher, and Hewitt. Thelma, seated at a table with the musicians, was nursing a glass of vermouth with a paper parasol on top. Saul ordered a double whisky and soda and munched all evening on oversalted pretzels. The lieutenant wasn't big on jazz, Latin jazz in particular. The only records he owned were those of Nat King Cole, Frank Sinatra, the Rat Pack, and Borscht Belt stars like Eddie Fischer and Carol Channing. Thelma Hammerstein was an alluring woman. A little over forty. Saul couldn't get why her midnight-blue eyes sparkled with pleasure. What had she done with her daughter's death? Was she hiding it? In what corner of her mind did she keep a place for the pain? These questions kept him from taking pleasure when he released himself into Thelma's body. "Is everything alright, sugar?" she'd asked when he got out of bed to light a cigarette and lean his elbows on the window-sill. She repeated the question, "Are you alright, sugar?" She got up, snuggled behind him. He felt her tiny breasts between his shoulder blades and her tiny dry hands running over his stomach. Outside, the heat was not letting up. Gantz even felt like everything was heating up more. He was sweating. Rivers of perspiration dripped from his armpits down his sides to Thelma's hands on his stomach and his sex. He lit another cigarette to put off going back to bed. Thelma's breath on his neck felt cloyingly sweet and the whole thing was unpleasant to him. The crows were ripping up garbage in the alley and the smell of rotten food wafted up the fire escape to his nostrils. Gantz turned around, caressed Thelma's cheek, tried to coax the strand that cut across her face back into place.

"You'd better go home," he whispered. "I could accompany you, if you'd like." It was a ridiculous offer. She lived in Newark and he in Brooklyn. It would take two hours at least to get there and back.

Thelma got dressed hastily, without a word, without a glance. Gantz saw her climb into a cab cruising for a fare at the corner of Nassau and Eckford. The lieutenant spent the rest of the night miserably drowning in a bottle of Bourbon and burning at the bottom of an ashtray while listening to Nat King Cole at the Sands.

It was too late. The stubborn detective from the 67th Street precinct hadn't seen Thelma's bottomless suffering brimming over until it was too late. He'd only grasped the full thrust of it when the thick fog had taken hold of the crazed woman's body at the corner of Nassau and Eckford.

Gantz could have caught her at the Van Gelder studio where he knew she worked. Tell her he was sorry. That he

needed her. That he desired her. That he'd been wrong.
That he hadn't understood at all the pretense of light-heart-
edness, the mambo break steps, the cocktails with parasols.
The lieutenant was all too familiar with the power of nightmares, waking up with his underwear drenched in sweat,
sheets clammy, eyelids puffy. They'd been familiar
company since his return from the battlefields in Korea.
Since the Pusan Perimeter and the piles of bodies. Since the
obscene sensation of his bayonet tearing through flesh.
Since the taste of burning men lodged deep in his throat,
stuck to the walls of his nostrils. So his regrets had little
weight. At any rate too little to cross the Hudson. Tal and
Thelma Hammerstein drowned in the amber liquid at the
bottom of his shot glass.

The swelter of September took over from the swelter of
August. The 28th was Yom Kippur. From the window of
his second-floor cubicle, Saul Gantz watched Jews walking
to services at Park East Synagogue. Like every year, he'd
have liked to go but didn't. On his Remington, typing
with two fingers in the finest police tradition, he drafted
the minutes of the interrogation he'd conducted with
Driscoll until the wee hours of the morning. A banal
affair of municipal corruption that ended with the murder
of an adulterous accountant from the tax department of
Providence in a striptease bar in Times Square. Gantz
hadn't found a replacement for Rosalinda. His apartment

was showing signs of this prolonged absence. A layer of dust exposed itself to the first ray of sunlight that peeked through the plastic slats of the venetian blinds. Newspapers and their weekend supplements piled up on the carpet. In what used to serve as a pantry, under the kitchen window, the lieutenant was amassing a collection of empty bottles that he no longer deigned to throw into the trash can in the backyard. In an attempt to relieve his increasingly frequent bouts of insomnia, he'd resumed his medical use of marijuana. He'd score a few blocks away under the pillars of the Brooklyn Queens Expressway. From a bedraggled war veteran back from Saigon.

When winter swept into the city without warning in mid-autumn, he knew nothing about the body of Thelma that the Jersey City police had recovered from the rocks of the Harborside Seawall.

SAUL'S LAMENT

It had been running around my mind for quite some time. How long? I couldn't say. At least two years, that's for sure. At the corner of Nassau and Eckford, when she'd left.

The image I hold in my mind is not of her face when we were making love or the sweat beading over her lip.

It's not even the dry softness of her hand. Of course I haven't forgotten . . . that would be idiotic. What I mean is that the first image that comes to mind, the one I see clearly, is of her silhouette. The silhouette I saw from my window when she climbed into the cab at the corner of Nassau and Eckford.

And then the smell of garbage that climbed up from the street, mixed with the sweet perfume she'd left lingering in my bedroom.

There are moments in life when things click, a conjuncture of circumstances. Fatalists will call it chance; mystics, providence. I call it the dybbuk, an obsession.

The waters were billowing gray vapors when we crossed the Hackensack River. Driscoll was steering the old Mercury with one hand, cigarette in his mouth, arm hanging out the window. With his dark aviator shades, his red sideburns, and his yellow short-sleeve shirt, he looked like a tough Irish mobster. We'd traveled to the other side of the Hudson for a joint investigation with the Garden State police. We were on our way back to the 67th Street precinct when I saw the sign for Englewood at a junction.

I asked Driscoll to drop me off and grabbed a cab to take me to the Van Gelder studios.

I wanted to confront Thelma's dybbuk. See how she'd aged, show her how I'd aged without her, try to repair my life, recapture what had haunted me and that I'd let slip away, who knows why. I have no gift for introspection. No inner couch, no impulse to go lie down on one at a shrink's.

When I got out of the cab at the studio, there was a small group of Black musicians flopped down on the front steps smoking cigarettes. Among them, there was one who looked like a lizard. Head resting against the concrete balustrade, he kept his eyes shut and seemed to be soaking up the sun like a tar pool. I practically had to step over them to reach the entrance.

In the hall, a rackety malfunctioning air-conditioner was grinding out waves of icy air. A girl with an afro was chatting on the phone. She looked my way without seeing me, absorbed in her conversation. Without the accoutrements of a cop, I was used to people looking right through me. It was probably the banal resignation of nondescript men that I betrayed on my face.

All things considered, the girl was nice. When she hung up, she flashed to me one of the loveliest smiles I'd ever seen. Two beautiful rows of slightly moist, sparkling teeth, which contrasted with her deep, husky voice.

"How can I help you?"

"I'd like to see Thelma."

"Does she work here?"

"Yes. With Mr. Van Gelder, I think."

"They're in the recording studio. Wait a minute, I see the musicians went outside. Maybe they're on a break. Let me check."

She picked up the phone.

"Rudy, a man . . . "

"Gantz, Saul Gantz."

"A Mr. Gantz is here to see Thelma. Oh! No, no, I didn't know . . . You think . . . I . . . "

She scratched her head with her pencil before telling me that Thelma had died over two years ago. She had the right expression and the right tone, which come to some people naturally when they deliver bad news.

I took it like a punch in the face. Like the bullet that struck Radioman Peterson between the eyes, right under his helmet, there, right next to me in the Pusan Perimeter.

I backed away toward the exit like a pious man from the Holy Ark. I sat on the stairs because my legs gave way under my weight. The sun was unsparing and yet I was racked by cold shivers I couldn't control. The lizard watched me through a half-closed eye.

I must have been there for a good half an hour when a guy came to sit by my side.

We spoke of Thelma. He knew her a little.

"Yeah, she was Van Gelder's assistant. Yeah, a terrific girl," he repeated several times. "A terrific girl who broke down after the death of her daughter. Tal, I think . . . "

"Yes, I was the one in charge of the investigation."

"And you didn't know that her mother committed suicide?"

"No. No, that I didn't know."

I spoke to him of Thelma and let my regrets and my remorse hang out. My dybbuk would remain a dybbuk.

He listened to me and then stood up and extended his hand. I couldn't see his face 'cause the sun had moved behind him.

"I'm Lee, Lee Konitz."

"Saul Gantz."

Rosalind, the cleaning lady, came back to work and my apartment on Eckford Street welcomed the winter as if a woman were taking care of me. I finally saw the panoramic view of the city from the top floor of the Pan Am Building. My weed dealer, the Vietnam veteran, died in an alley and Lieutenant Driscoll ditched me to become captain in the Garment District. Doc Johnson, the coroner, divorced the stripper. He also lost five thousand dollars in a game of Black Jack in Atlantic City.

As all things must change, and so on and so forth, without much consequence on the world, the young beardless rabbi of Park East Synagogue was replaced by an even younger one, with the look of a Columbia University student of philosophy just back from a trip to Kathmandu.

From the top of the Pan Am Building, on a foggy day, you can't see Harborside Bay and you can barely make out the New York Steam Company smokestack.

Lee Konitz came out with a new album. I went to listen to it at a record store near Macy's. On the cover, you see him with his sax slung over his shoulder and also the lizard who plays double bass. I flipped the cover and saw that one of the tracks on the B side was called *Saul's Lament*.

I put the LP back and walked out of the overheated store. I lit a cigarette, blocking the wind with my coat collar. I spat out the smoke far above my head.

I don't like jazz.

THE GREAT AMERICAN DISASTER

When the cops brought Dad home, he was all mocking smiles and proud of himself. I should have known that things would start unraveling. Instead, I laughed.

First I laughed because his getup was funny. Picture this! He'd put on his army pea jacket and all the medals he'd collected in Korea. He'd protected his bald head with a blue cap from the last Democratic primaries of George McGovern and, under his pea jacket, he was wearing an orange Hawaiian shirt with blue palm trees. To top it off, he'd slipped into Mom's burgundy skirt, the one she wore on cleaning days before Passover.

When they apprehended him in front of Lincoln Center, he struck the police officers with his sign, demanding respect for his rights and the First Amendment. On the sign in question he threatened Tricky Dicky with the wrath of the people and he shouted slogans against the war in Vietnam between two trumpet blasts. We had just celebrated, two days before, his forty-fifth birthday.

I was home studying for exams with my girlfriend Janet. Actually we were busier making out than boning up on the writings of Thoreau or the industrial development of the Midwest when the fuzz brought Dad back in his getup.

Janet ushered my father into the kitchen, made him a cup of tea which she served with his favorite cinnamon cookies while I endured admonishments, sanctimonious lecturing, and threats of hospitalization from the police.

We sat down and watched the Johnny Carson show on TV together, then put my father to sleep, making sure he took his pills. Janet and I were eighteen. We'd known each other since elementary school in Greenpoint and never once did we doubt that we would end our lives together.

We listened to a Grateful Dead album, smoked a joint, and agreed that things might take a more serious turn for my father next time round. We also agreed that although these last three years, since the death of my mother in fact, hadn't been a picnic with him, yet the days, weeks, and years to come were going to be more challenging still.

Hard to say what had messed him up most: Korea or Mom's death.

When he'd come back from the 38th parallel, he was a wreck. He no longer slept without nightmares rattling him. As time passed, he'd be overcome by tremors or paralyzed by sudden fits of wordless tears. Thanks to Mom, who'd found a job for him in a law firm, he managed to hold it together. Obviously, there was no question of him arguing a case. He presented himself as the firm's dusty but indispensable constitutional authority. His colleagues called him to the rescue to clarify gray areas, identify loopholes, find procedural flaws.

When I was a kid, Saturdays my mother and I would go visit him in his office, a dim cubicle lined with reddish-brown leather-bound books. His table was cluttered with papers, notebooks, teacups full of soggy cigarette butts, and he, in shirtsleeves, was overjoyed to see us.

We'd bring him apple strudel and a thermos of tea and we'd drink and eat together amid the chaos of legal documents, leaning against tottering piles of gray cloth files and imitation-wood cardboard folders.

We'd always lived in Brooklyn in a three-room apartment filled with the smell of fried food. Ruben's joint at the corner fried all kinds of food. Since my only exposure to his food was olfactive, I imagined that he fried up just about anything: whales, swallows, scorpions, cats, and onions of course, 'cause everything had to be served with a bucketful of onions. Which justified the daily delivery, at the crack of dawn, of a huge sack of them in the stairwell.

Ruben was our landlord and a distant cousin of my mother, which is why it never occurred to us to protest against the stench which was as natural to us as exhaust fumes, the swelter of summer, and the gusts of sea breeze that wafted up the river and Kent Avenue. And then, as Mom would say, when the stink became intolerable, "What's the big deal? Don't we eat onions?" And it was true, so why complain?

We had crumbs of family on my mother's side and an Aunt Mirele, a phantom aunt, on my father's. Back from the fighting in Pusan, Dad's only friend was Saul, a comrade in arms, a neurasthenic cop who treated his neurasthenia with all sorts of crap. We weren't fussy. We took what came our way. Saul was not warm but he was our Sunday entertainment, a "special guest star" on our own shows. To my ears, he was an inexhaustible source of information about the city and the monsters that peopled it. As a child, he was my Eliot Ness; as a teenager, my Columbo.

He and my father listened religiously to Nat King Cole, windows closed to muffle the sound system at Ruben's who held "deep-fry dance parties" on Sundays. We weren't poor. We could have lived in a swankier neighborhood than this one that exhausted itself integrating, decade after decade, waves of new immigrants that wiped out the traces of the preceding waves. Ruben's greasy spoon and our family were leftovers from the forties. My father's condition was why we never moved and, in the end, it suited us alright.

My mother worked at a Pan Am travel agency specialized in flights to Mexico and the Caribbean. The redbrick building was located at the corner of Anchorage and Plymouth, under the piers of the Manhattan Bridge.

Saturday afternoon, I took piano lessons in a handsome building on John Street, overlooking the river and the electric power plant. Afterwards, I'd go pick up Mom at six o'clock on the dot, between John Street and Plymouth, a memory curiously mixed with Liszt and mambo.

Saul and my father formed an odd couple. Often in silence, they'd share beers, clinking the bottles with each new round. Although I never heard them speak about their war, the one in Vietnam came up in all their conversations. In low voices, like conspirators, they commented on the articles that my father, true to his monomania with archiving, would cut out, staple, and classify compulsively during the week.

When my mother died, there were not many of us at the cemetery. Saul Gantz, Ruben, Madeline, a Pan Am colleague, Dad's boss, *the* Samuel Goldstein of Goldstein, MacArthur, and Miller, Janet and I. The Jews put stones on the mound; the others, carnations that Janet handed out. Dad wasn't there. An ambulance from the Presbyterian's psychiatric unit came for him during the night.

Mom dead, Dad hospitalized, it was the first time I came home to an empty apartment. Janet stayed over. We made love for the first time. It was the night of Mom's burial.

Papa left the hospital with a zombie treatment. Back home, he went straight to bed. For a week, he came out of his room only to go to the bathroom and put in the sink the dinner platter Janet had made for him. Back from college, I'd buy him his favorite hot dog, the one from Dizzie's, speckled with cumin, smeared with mustard, and smothered in sauerkraut.

I had confidence. He was eating his hot dogs. Once, toward the end of the week, I even heard a "thank you" from behind the door.

It wasn't until a couple of months after Mom's death that Aunt Mirele, Dad's older sister whom I only knew by name, decided it was finally time to meet the family.

It was a Sunday afternoon. Saul Gantz had brought an apple pie, which we munched on while watching a Yankee game on TV. Aunt Mirele? Well, what can I say? The surprise was total, a bit less so for Dad, to be sure, but Saul, Janet, and I were blown away.

The good woman, my aunt that is, must have been in her fifties, short, pudgy, shapeless. Beneath a tight-fitting brown headscarf, a fringe of synthetic hair. Beneath the fringe, two black eyes like ice picks in some pulp thriller. I'd seen women like that when I walked through Williamsburg, gray and black shadows, heads covered with hats, wigs, or scarves, saddled with strollers and kids. She didn't stay long. She embraced her brother, whispered three or four words in Yiddish, left her address and telephone number on a pile of articles cut out of the *New York Times* and the *Post*. She nodded politely to us before scurrying away like a big gray mouse in crepe soles and abandoning my father to a fit of wordless tears.

Dad never went back to work. Samuel Goldstein, his boss, made sure we would not be in need. And we never were.

To "foster his awareness of the world around him," the therapist from the Presbyterian unit encouraged us to indulge my father's impulses. The living room, rather quickly when I look back at it now, was turned into a store-house for his archives on Vietnam. Janet and I would bring back all the journals and student newsletters that had the misfortune of crossing our paths between Marcy Avenue and Broadway-Lafayette. Visitors would have been taken aback, rightly so, if we had had any, by the sight of the new furnishings, especially the humongous metallic-gray office-type cabinet that formed a monstrous obstacle at the center of the room, and the smaller filing cabinet with a fluorescent label marked My Lai Massacre and shelves bearing all the dates of the great American disaster. Saul was no stranger to feeding Dad's obsessions, and for good reason, since he shared a number of them. These secret obsessions about Korea that made him neurasthenic and my father insane.

The sudden appearance of my aunt Mirele, as I immediately sensed, triggered upheavals for the family. My father still kept quiet about how the war had ripped him apart, but now he was forced to open up about his real identity.

I wasn't an idiot. From a very early age I'd developed a certain awareness of my unspoken origins.

Primo, my White father was Jewish. Our last name, Kagan, made that crystal clear, as did a number of fetishistic hygienic practices such as the major spring cleaning around Passover, or the Yiddish expressions that mysteriously peppered my father's vocabulary and trickled into my mother's and mine.

Secondo, my mother was a Black woman from Port-au-Prince. We lived in a Black neighborhood and my complexion bore witness to something so out of the ordinary, in those days, that it sometimes triggered hostility as much from my Black brothers as from my White ones.

With the sudden arrival of Mirele in our lives and the admission, a quarter of a century after the fact, of my father's excommunication from his family, I realized that my Jewish brothers were no better than the others. I was but a *schvartze*, a Black, to them; my father, a renegade.

I accepted being half Black, I accepted being half Jewish. As for Papa, he stopped wearing his vintage pea jacket, stopped cutting out articles on the monstrosities of the Vietnam War, stopped shaving too. Six months later, he was wearing a black velvet yarmulke and was going to services at his childhood shul, six blocks from our apartment. As the living room was emptied of its metal furnishings, it was repopulated with bound mystical-kabbalistic volumes.

Saul Gantz, who'd come to look like Ben Gazzara in Eugene O'Neill's *Hughie*, eventually admitted to us that my father's headlong return to his roots bore more resemblance to a new rebellion than to repentance. Day after day, in a Hassidic synagogue, he howled the kaddish of orphans and widowers like a devastating indictment against God.

It all came to a head on April 30, 1975. At around five in the morning, Janet thought her waters broke. Everything was ready. I'd borrowed Dad's sausage-shaped khaki duffel for Janet's toiletries and change of clothing. For a week it had been sitting there in the foyer like a dachshund draft stopper decorated with the spangled banner and spots of rifle grease.

Speaking of water, when I came back into the bedroom, I found Janet prostrate, her head between her hands, and, in the sheets, a piece of the placenta, as big as a slice of veal liver. We didn't take the duffel.

At nine in the morning, I was the brand-new dad of a little girl of barely four and a half pounds. At ten, I was a widower. Janet's body had emptied itself of blood and the doctors at Presbyterian couldn't do a thing.

Gantz drove me back home. I heard him whispering with my father behind the bedroom wall. The tranquilizers I'd been given plunged me into a numbness as black as an oil slick on the East River. The sun was crashing down on the other side of the river and smashing against the slats of the blinds, casting blood-red bars on the walls.

I must have been sleeping when CBS announced the fall of Saigon.

FORESTER OAKWOOD

"You know very well what I want, Forester."

The Forester in question, a sturdy fellow of around twenty, was staring at the tips of his two-tone shoes.

"You know very well," Duke continued striking the lid of the piano with his hand. "But you can't read a fucking score. Damn you, Forester! Go find Billy and ask him for your money."

Without batting an eyelash, Forester put his trombone back into its cracked cardboard case and closed the score he couldn't decipher. He didn't bother to look at the guys in the orchestra. Gonsalves, ass glued to his seat, pushed it back to let him pass between him and the music stand. The chair made an unpleasant grating sound that accompanied Forester Oakwood's exit.

Mr. Strayhorn was nowhere to be found. So Forester left the studios without pocketing the money he was owed.

What's there to do at one in the morning in Englewood, New Jersey, without a penny, when you live on the east side of the river? First you sit down on the steps outside the studio, light a cigarette, look at the stars in the dark moonless sky, then the line of lights on the Palisades Parkway. You spit out the smoke as high as possible. You flick the butt as far as possible, following with your eyes the swirling embers for as long as possible and the sparks it sends flying when it hits the asphalt. The night was hot. A stifling, steaming, vegetal stench cut across the ground rising from the park and the Hudson.

Three-quarters of an hour later, the young man started across the Washington Bridge on foot. There was an uninterrupted flow of cars. In passing, some of the convertibles, stocked with pinups and roughnecks, pumped out the sounds of merengue and cha-cha-cha.

On the other side, Washington Heights slept in an orange fog.

Forester didn't see anyone walking in the opposite direction and no one was going his way either. Under the pier of the bridge, directly above the red lighthouse, he opened the case, took out his trombone, and began playing Curtis Fuller's score from "Blue Train."

He knew by heart Fuller's speed of delivery, his staccatos, and his prodigious ability to leap over four full octaves with the greatest of ease.

When officers O'Riley and Stacchini found the trombone under the east pier at seven in the morning, they could easily imagine the dislocated body of its owner, eyes open, lying on the moss-covered rocks of Fort Washington or, perhaps, drifting on the banks of Fort Lee or Edgewater, gorged with foul-smelling water. It wouldn't have been the first time, because of the currents and boat backwash.

But let's go back three hundred minutes in time, to the exact moment when Forester, still standing on the safe side of the guardrail, might have yielded, after a final glissando, to the ineluctable theory of gravity or an ill-conceived swim.

It was a quarter to two. The Duke was tired. He'd unbuttoned the collar of his starched shirt and had collapsed into the warm leather seat in the rear of the Dodge. He'd stretched out his long legs and was trying to catch the rare particles of fresh air penetrating into the car. Herb, who saw his boss nodding off in the rearview mirror, came from Portland on the West Coast and didn't like these New York summer nights.

It was so muggy that the sounds seemed muffled by a hot, spongy snow. When he drove the Dodge onto the glistening tongue of the Washington Bridge, a foul-smelling but cooler blast of air was blowing toward the ocean. With his thumb and forefinger, Herb peeled his sticky white shirt from his skinny torso. He felt the sweat trickling down from his armpits to his ribs, then running down his sides, before getting lost in the meanders and folds of the overly loose pinstripe pants he'd borrowed from a buddy.

When he finally reached Manhattan, he spied the young trombonist whom Duke had just fired an hour before. In fact, Herb heard him before seeing him. The kid was shooting into his horn the interrogative notes of "Blue Train." Da da da da da—da? Da da da da da—da? The same piercing question asked in all tones and that only finds its answer in the clear and luminous edginess of Coltrane's sax.

It must have been ten to two when Paul Gonsalves's European convertible passed the Dodge, honking its horn. Already the swelter of Manhattan crept over the last few feet of the suspension bridge's asphalt. Herb had spent a long time in the Van Gelder Studio parking lot ogling the saxophonist's automobile, a gem in chrome and chocolate, cream seats, mahogany dashboard. An amazing piece of machinery that he'd have loved to drive, to take his girlfriend Flora to Coney Island or, better yet, to the Hamptons, where the wealthy live, yeah, the Hamptons, or, better yet, to Newport with the boss.

Earlier, Paul Gonsalves had tossed his sax on the back seat. He'd been the last to leave the studios that night. A stiff shot of firewater before leaving with a studio technician who'd come to wake him up.

The bastards! They'd all run off, leaving him on the recording-room sofa. He'd dozed off, just for a moment, watching the display of Thelma the assistant's smooth legs.

It was so hot. The sticky air, as he drove along the Hudson River to the Washington Bridge turnoff, clung to his face like spiderweb. He cursed when he had to slow down on the bridge. "Goddamnit! At this fuckin' time a'night! Why aren't these bougees bunkin' in their cribs!"

In the end, he couldn't have slept that long, he realized, as he caught up with the boss's Dodge. Driving alongside, he gestured to Duke's chauffeur with the back of his left hand pressed against his right cheek to show he'd been sleeping. Herb, who'd rolled down his window, responded in kind, pointing his thumb at his boss, out like a light on the back seat.

Did the honker hear Forester's trombone? Did he even glimpse at him, standing, his back to the guardrail? If he didn't hear him, it's a pity. Gonsalves liked the little guy, plenty of wind and courage. He blew fine sounds outta that metal! The boss had been too hard on him. The kid had been too rebellious, and it wasn't the night for rebels.

After overtaking the big Dodge, as heavy as a cow, he headed south on the Henry Hudson. He groped for his flask of Bacardi on the passenger seat while, in Englewood, Joe locked up the Van Gelder studios.

Left-hand Joe, nicknamed for the stump that emerged like a shank of ham from his T-shirt, put his cigarette down on the curbstone to lock the double-glass door. The booze didn't boost his precision or patience. His fingers fumbled finding the slot to insert the new-model flat key.

Between his teeth, in a trail of drool, his curses, complaints, and insults collided. Against everything and the kitchen sink. Korea, General MacArthur, the goddamn arm left in Daejeon, and these fucking flat keys and these tiny fucking locks!

At two in the morning, Joe, who had his crib in a motel on Sherwood Avenue, less than half a mile from the studios, hit the sack fully clothed. Staring at the cracks in the ceiling, he regretted having introduced the Forester kid to Mr. Strayhorn. The Duke had fired the kid and now he must be really wasted.

And yet Joe had a good ear. He'd heard a lot of horns since he'd been working as a technician at Van Gelder's. Forester Oakwood was a champ! Pity that the kid overdid his thing to impress the boss.

When Left-Hand Joe finally closed his heavy boozed eyelids, Thelma was putting her clothes back on at the corner of Nassau and Eckford. Behind her, Saul, in an undershirt, seated on the unmade bed, asked if she wanted him to accompany her home. Tears were welling up in her eyes, so she didn't answer. All she wanted was to get the hell out of there.

Thelma climbed into a cab to get back home. To her place, on the good side of the river. As her taxi passed the tall outline of Yankee Stadium on her right, it drove past the Duke's big, dark Dodge without her seeing it.

It was two forty-five when the limo parked in front of the corner flatiron building that housed Minton's Playhouse, Harlem's best bebop club. Herb stepped out to open the door to the old man, beating to it the slick doorman who was hoping to get a big-ass tip.

The Duke climbed out like an aristo. He smoothed his slick-backed hair with the palm of his hand, adjusted the red handkerchief in his pocket, rebuttoned his double-breasted pinstripe jacket, and, turning back to the Dodge, shot out:

"You getting out, Forester? Get a move on it. Here's where ya'll be able to play the rebel. Your night begins here, kiddo."

A SON, NORTH OF 110TH STREET

"Going out, Ma."

Six months from now, he won't even bother telling me.

The mother stopped the movement of her hands along the edge of the sink. The lukewarm water was running over the two dirty plates and the leftover breaded fish, mayonnaise, and ketchup.

He repeated, "Going out, Ma," to make sure she'd heard him over the sound of the TV and the gurgling faucet. She didn't answer because she was weary, and it wouldn't do any good. She heard the door slam shut behind her baby like a question to which she had no answer.

On the floor was the paper cup of the extra-large Coke that Winston had lobbed toward the garbage in imitation of Willis Reed's free throws. A few years ago, it would have been enough to say, "Winston, pick that up," and the kid might have cheekily tried another shot, from a different angle perhaps, but he'd have picked it up.

41

She was still young, for Christ's sake, and yet her back was as stiff as an old lady's. The cup had left a dark spot on the linoleum. Damned heat! It made everything so much tougher. She dampened the nearly dry sponge and got down on her hands and knees to clean the spot, already as sticky as caramel forming at the bottom of a saucepan.

With the kitchen tidied up, she switched off the neon light, leaving the windowless alcove in total darkness. She remembered how, not so long ago, she'd leave the light on for her "young'uns," Tyler and Winston, because they were scared of the dark. *Back then they were scared of the dark*, she repeated in her mind with rueful irony.

The night had slowly infiltrated the living room. A doddery fan kept up a pretense of coolness. It was Thursday. *The Dean Martin Show* had begun. Usually when she watched it, she drifted into the mind-quieting hypnotic state that the producers of the show were seeking. Tonight, she turned down the sound.

Was Joe watching Dean Martin on NBC?

Mechanically, like nearly everything she'd done since she'd come home from work, she started dusting the furniture. To wipe down the TV, she had to move the three-photo frame that sat atop the box. In the center was a picture of Joe before he left for Korea, Tyler on his father's right, Winston on his left. Tyler was a frail child. He hadn't been cut out for a neighborhood like this. She put the frame down before eyeballing Winston's face.

How stupid! Losing an arm! It wasn't lost, it had been ripped off, stolen. MacArthur, Kim Il-sung, Mao, all those motherfuckers had ripped out his soul.

Joe thought he was nothing and nobody when he came home. At first, she didn't understand what being nothing and nobody could mean. Even a shadow is something. Even a shadow with an arm amputated is something. And then, with the alcohol, the shadow proved to be amputated of its soul and she finally understood that her husband had become nothing and nobody. He was nothing and nobody when he came home drunk at all hours. He was nothing and nobody when he looked at his sons with the glassy eyes of inner exile. He didn't have his right arm anymore so the man who was nothing and nobody beat her with his left.

And then one night, also a summer night, she kicked out the stranger who'd come back from Korea, he, his medals, his stump, his eyes like a catfish washed aground, and every inch of his body that exuded alcohol and terror.

Winston hadn't come home.

The street was nearly silent by now, save for the hum of the city and the sporadic echo in the distance of an automatic weapon. A streetlight flickered and you could see in its trembling halo a swarm of frantic midges.

She'd raised him and Tyler alone and then one Wednesday Tyler had gone to Marcus for piano lessons as he did every Wednesday. All week, he'd been practicing a mazurka by Scriabin, in the backroom at Barry's. On the way to Marcus's, Tyler had crossed paths with some junkies, zombies from Saint Nicholas bars who were terrorizing a couple of grocers, ransacking their store with as much fear as malice. Then came the arrival of an NYPD patrol on the scene, the flight, and an exchange of fire. One bullet, among the dozens, hit Tyler in the head.

Two cops in uniform, one White, one Black, had broken the news to her.

It was customary in those days to explain this kind of tragedy with a fatalistic, "wrong guy at the wrong place" shrug and it wasn't true! It was a lie, it was cowardly. She resented this collective resignation that reached pinnacles of abjection in the fervent Hallelujahs in church and the conventional preaching by smooth-talking reverends.

"Oh sister! Oh sister," the old mamas tried to comfort her with tears, caressing hands, sweets from Gus's, soda pop, and "Jesus is welcoming him into His grace." Sunk into the sofa, with their fascinator hats and their gloved hands resting over their fat bellies and flowery dresses, they believed they were soothing her pain with their gospel humming.

Winston had still not come home.

The TV tube crackled, burned reckless insects in mid-flight. It was one in the morning, and she hadn't wanted to undress.

Closing her eyelids, she summoned up a clear picture of the cop, the white guy, who came that day. Sergeant Gantz still had his arms and legs, yet she saw in his eyes the same look as in Joe's. It spoke of despair, inner exile, vulnerability, devastation. It was as if a film of other images, hidden deep in his skull, masked the colorful reality of the world. He too must have thought that he was nothing and nobody. But he was straight with her, not more, not less, merely a White officer come to break the news to a Negro woman that her Negro son was dead, killed by White cops in a Negro neighborhood. Or maybe it was all those secret images that made this man and all those with the same look in their eyes inaccessible to life itself.

Winston hadn't come home.

She finished her coffee. In the darkness of the kitchen, she rinsed her glass and the coffee pot under the lukewarm trickle from the faucet. She must have dozed off. The fluorescent hands of the small clock marked five o'clock and dawn was already poking its feverish nose through the window.

When life is butchered by the Good Lord's great knife, suddenly human beings, the women in particular, tend to discover mystical inclinations. The men are more likely to be like Joe and Saul, and turn themselves inside out like a dishwashing glove, with all the grease, the shit, the water, and the soap on the inside, and those goddamn fingertips that you can't prize out of the palm and that form strange fingerless stumps. She hadn't turned to God, hadn't even questioned him. She hadn't sought the cloying consolation of the church or of charitable organizations, nor the redemptive and vindictive rage of the Black Panthers.

With the light beginning to strike the cracked ceiling, she tried to lower the wooden blinds but, this time, finally, the goddamn frayed cord snapped, and the blind came crashing down, sharp and precise like the blade of a guillotine.

She was alone. Her life resembled Lennox Avenue after the great looting. Devastated it remained because an avenue is there to bring people to their address and her life; well, her life had brought Winston to tonight.

At ten after five, she closed the door behind her as if she were suddenly answering a long-unanswered question.

The sky to the west was open, clear, and bright. Behind her, it was black, laden with a liberating storm. The street-light was still crackling over her head, in its by now useless light.

She strode down the lifeless street straight as an arrow, fists clenched. She was going to find Winston, bring him back home. A fresh cup of coffee awaited the son on the cracked marble of the kitchen.

HOME RUN

On his desk, softly lit by a green opaline lamp, prominently placed in a very dark wood frame, was a black-and-white photo of a home run, *his* home run. He took more than a little pride in this snapshot featured in the *Brooklyn Herald*. A spectacular dive onto home plate that had kicked up the chalk and dry grass of the Stuyvesant High School stadium.

It coincided with his graduation and news of his admission to Ezra Dickson as a first-year social science and economics major. Ezra Dickson hadn't been his first choice, but it wasn't bad at all. Columbia University was still practicing a clandestine *numerus clausus* for Jews.

To celebrate his excellent end-of-year results, his father had bought him a used 1947 Plymouth De Luxe, as black as a hearse, with a red-lead-colored left rear fender. His dad, who owned only a run-down pickup for his business, sacrificed himself with loving admiration in a way that flattered Joseph as much as it terrified him by the weight of hope and expectations that Menachem Rappaport invested in him.

The whole neighborhood called his father Nach'm. He was a small-time kosher grocer in Brighton Beach. The store was a narrow rectangle that spilled out onto the sidewalk under a tarpaulin awning mounted on two patriotically tri-colored poles. Nach'm, who was a lousy shopkeeper but an ingenious little guy, five feet tall, had devised this removable overhang to protect from the elements the vegetable crates on the right and the fruit crates on the left.

The actual choice of fruits and vegetables that Joseph's father proposed to his customers was very limited. If you weren't interested in potatoes or beets or cabbage or corn or Golden Delicious apples, then the Rapp Grocery wasn't for you. Then again, the grocery never pretended to be a branch of Macy's in Brighton Beach, just a small shop in a neighborhood of poor immigrants from Eastern Europe.

Only once did Joseph Herschel Rappaport recall having seen strawberries on offer outside his father's store. The bright-red fruit had been the pride of both father and son for three days running. Alas, no one in the neighborhood had the means to buy them. The strawberries at the bottom of the pile rotted and began dripping, forming trickles of blood on the sidewalk, sticky rivulets that passersby stepped over, grumbling. The strawberries that did not end up in the garbage were turned into jam for home use. A net loss of seven dollars for the grocer who refused, that whole "strawberry year," to put a spoonful of jam into his mouth.

The grocer eked out a living as best he could, enough at any rate to feed, clothe, and educate his sole offspring, the son of his old age. There was no dearth of poor people, and their sons were the best-protected human species in the neighborhood. Here, in the six-block radius of buildings, every *yiddische tate* saw his progeny as the treasure, the hope, the promise of better days.

In the summer, Joseph helped out at the grocery. As a child, he was put in charge of the canned food, arranging and dusting the cans and counting them at the end of the day. As a teenager, he ran errands. As a young adult, the summer before he entered Ezra Dickson, his father entrusted him for the first time with the use of the abacus and a brand-new dark-wood National Cash Register.

The grocery smelled of fresh sawdust, herrings, onions, and cinnamon. Once a week, on Fridays, these overpowering scents were rounded off by whiffs of Star Wax that the mother used to polish the counter.

Joseph met all his father's expectations. He'd been Reb Rosensky's favorite student in heder, a studious and obedient pupil in Windermere Crescent, and then in Stuyvesant high school.

At Ezra Dickson University, Joseph joined the Jewish fraternity, the baseball team, the debate team, the Democratic Party, and the community of tormented virgins. He shared his dorm room with George Hammerstein, a red-head in his second year of law. A nerd from Newark who'd come back Sunday nights from a weekend at home, reeking of ammoniac and fumes from his father's tannery. No matter how much he doused himself with Aqua Velva, only the Tuesday-morning shower would dispel the stench that clung to him. Joseph got into the habit of exiling himself to left-handed pitcher Aaron Falk's room from Sunday night to Tuesday morning.

That was probably the year with the most Jews on Ezra Dickson campus. Denied access to Columbia, the brainy kids invaded the university, snapping up the scholarships for meritorious students. This demographic shift had the effect of resolving some of the ethnic and religious tensions between fraternities through an exchange of punches between the Jewish frats. The dean had to put all his diplomatic skills to bear to restore a semblance of order and save the season from the baseball and Greco-Roman wrestling teams that were knocking the crap out of each other in the dressing rooms. The totally judenrein basket-ball and football teams had no such problem, but every Thursday and Saturday they were the laughingstock of all New York State. The university, which had had in the past three NFL stars and a first-rate long-range shooting guard, was being trounced in the lower divisions. Notwith-standing Joseph Herschel Rappaport's best intentions, baseball was not having a great season either, even though it wasn't quite as disastrous as the union of one-handed goys: six weeks in a row without a home run.

*

Truman had just relieved General MacArthur of his command. As America became mired in the war, the campus split into pro- and anti-Truman camps. During a meeting organized by supporters of the fired general in response to the ticker-tape parade in New York City, Hammerstein succeeded in convincing his studious dormmate to join the Democratic chapters on campus and in Carthage, Tompkins County, New York.

In his senior year, he was within a hair's breath of being elected president of the community of tormented virgins, when he met Gena Baker-Stone, a busty shikse from Port Jefferson, Long Island. Gena from Port Jefferson was the grandchild on her father's side of an abolitionist in the House of Representatives and, on her mother's, of a Southern textile dynasty.

It was love at first sight for the young virgin from Brighton Beach, which was hardly the case for the elegant C-cup blond from Long Island. Height, first of all: Gena towered over Joseph by a good inch and a half. And then, abolitionist though the paternal lineage of her family was, it would be fair to say that the Baker-Stones were what you might call enlightened anti-Semites and fervent Baptists.

Enlightened anti-Semites, in Joseph's view, were those who didn't refuse you entry to their home, would invite you over for a July 4 barbecue on their lawn overlooking the bay, trust a Jewish banker, read the *New York Times*, vote for Adlai Stevenson against Ike, listen to the music of George Gershwin and Benny Goodman, and yet teach their daughters about the dangers of consorting with a son of Israel. Later, from some of the conversations between the two, Joseph (whom she called Joe) was given to understand that for Mrs. Baker-Stone, Jews (not all of course) resorted to all sorts of ruses to come to their predatory sexual ends. All of which was said with a hint of a Southern drawl and a knowing smile.

As he waited for Gena to finally notice him, he practiced onanism with all the guilt and shame of a little yid raised in the backroom of a kosher grocery in Brighton Beach. His roommate, George Hammerstein, who'd finished his law studies, joined the campaign team of John Kennedy who'd just entered the senatorial race. Joe Rappaport didn't like the young Catholic representative. His love affair with the Democrats was with Eleanor, Stevenson, and the New York liberals, not with the son of a family that had been in bed with the mob during Prohibition and was friendly with Joseph McCarthy, the rabid, loathsome crusader against communism.

This stance distanced him for a time from his romantic goal. Gena, who still hadn't noticed him, also joined the Boston campaign headquarters and the Kennedy groupies.

On June 30, 1953, on the lawn of the campus, Joseph Herschel Rappaport, along with two hundred other graduates, threw his cap in the air as his parents watched with tear-filled eyes. On July 27, 1953, he let out a huge sigh of relief. The Korean War came to an end and, with it, the anticipated tragedy of his future conscription.

*

The summer of '53 was a strange dance. Early Monday and Thursday morning, he'd go to the wholesale market, load the old pickup to the hilt so his father could fulfil his most cherished desire, join the minyan, and listen to the Torah reading at the *Shaharit* services. He'd help the grocer until noon. Then, notwithstanding his mother's persistent efforts to gorge him with food at lunch, hoping she could talk him into a nap, so he'd stay close to her, he'd climb into his 1947 Plymouth De Luxe and head to Manhattan to meet up with George in Greenwich Village. On one of his first trips to the disreputable Village, he stumbled upon the lovely Gena and all his fantasies about her body sprung back to life.

The summer of '53 was like a dance, a whirlwind, a waltz, a drunken spree. The sun, the beach, the political sparring in the Village bars, the anxiety about being drafted, so near and so far, the sweet fatigue of sleepless nights, and the first coffee at the wholesale market. And then, that escapade to Port Jefferson, the boat at full sail to the Hamptons, the midnight swim, the coolness of the water and of her skin. Everything was perfectly organized and arranged, like in a technicolor film that a Hollywood director might have called *The Summer of '53* or *The Graduate*.

Mrs. Baker-Stone watched her daughter from behind the living-room windows. The first kiss that Joe exchanged with the Port Jefferson heir took place, as a result, far from her inquisitive gaze, in the covered tennis court. The girl's lips glistened with her saliva and hot drops of sweat beaded down her cheeks, flushed as much from athletic exertion as from emotions. His eyes were so close to hers he could see his reflection in her pupils. He could feel the erect tips of her breasts under her jersey. She slipped her tongue into his mouth, fresh and flavorful as a stick of Wrigley's spearmint gum. She let him caress her big firm breasts which he imagined white, and she caressed his crotch through the fabric of his shorts. Without delay he released his semen, suppressing a grimace of pleasure that he supposed unbecoming. This first "social" ejaculation produced by the hand of a third party opened the inevitable Pandora's box in the noodle of the Jew from Brooklyn, and out sprung, in no particular order, a peak of guilt, a surge of excitement, the faces of Reb Rosensky and of his mother, and his father Nach'm's small, square hand smacking his cheek when caught smoking with the Alterman boy in the backyard of the grocery. Out sprung, too, the first lines of the "Song of Songs" which, as a teenager sitting in the Ocean Parkway shul, used to give him a hard-on: "Let him kiss me with the kisses of his mouth—for your love is more delightful than wine." Not to mention the lines: "I am my beloved's, And my beloved is mine, Who feeds his flock among the lilies."

Although Joseph was not a bookworm (*Moby Dick* and Emily Dickinson's poetry had left him cold), he'd grasped all the erotic poetry of the sacred text attributed to King Solomon. All this leaped into his head at the very moment when, in his underpants, his swollen member released twenty-two years of virginity and ecstatic ambitions.

In October '53, right after the festival of Sukkoth, Joseph Herschel Rappaport walked into the Brooklyn Veterans Hospital and emerged Private Joe Rappaport, then Corporal Joe H. Rapp. A cushy job! A damned cushy job that Gena's father had secured for him with a single call to D.C. The scion of an abolitionist family would have done anything for his darling daughter, and hadn't this little kike graduated first in his class?

Mrs. Baker-Stone could have strangled him when she learned what he'd done for Joseph. The idiot, the oblivious fool, what had he done? What she wanted was to see this Hebe from Brighton Beach sent somewhere remote in

Montana or Iowa, for lack of a good war on the other side of the planet, say in Indochina, millions of miles from New York State, light years away from Gena.

Joe went back home every night. No barracks for him. Since public transit was free for conscripts, he left his Plymouth De Luxe under a tarp in the alley by the shop. In the morning, he would make the trip across the borough from south to north in a bumpy and fuming pre-war bus, packed with grandmothers like so many wizened effigies o the shtetl, perfumed secretaries in nylon stockings, and workers asleep after a night of labor.

Joseph relished this ride beyond reason. He loved watching the neighborhoods growing wealthier as the bus made its way north. The kid from Brighton Beach, the youngster who grew up in substandard tenements and sand, everywhere sand, and salt, everywhere salt, on the rhododendrons, on the leprous lawns, in the ditches, in the gutters, on all the fire-escape railings, that salty and sweaty urchin with sticky hair, the child from Brighton Beach loved this affluence ten blocks from his home. The trimmed trees, the manicured gardens, the lawns grassier than a meadow in Wyoming, and the women, the beautiful women, bareheaded, in nylon stockings, cigarettes in their mouths.

He found that the uniform suited him. Before his ten o'clock rounds, he'd spend a few minutes checking in the bathroom mirror that his tie was properly knotted, his spats adjusted, and his cap slanted over his left ear, in the purest mock-casual U.S. Army tradition. Joseph worked as a postmaster at the Veterans Hospital. He sorted and distributed the mail to military personnel with two of his mates: Dalton Brown, a Black guy from Tuscaloosa, Alabama; and Sergeant Zak Burns, a White guy from Tabiona, Utah, some hick town of a hundred sixty-seven souls and a Church of Jesus Christ of Latter-Day Saints.

Burns had served in Korea, and it wasn't clear whether he should be counted among the staff or among the wackos. He didn't talk, ate by himself, propped against the fridge as if he were guarding the door. He sorted and distributed the mail: two hours and forty-five minutes to sort his two bags, two hours for the distribution, wings B and C plus the command offices. A 250-pound machine with hands as big as a baseball glove, clumsy as someone using two baseball gloves instead of hands. His mitts were so impressive that one day a sergeant who was a bit of a moron, with the sense of humor of a moron, unabashedly asked him if he could see his dick when he jerked off. Zak Burns had a strange reaction that deterred witnesses to the scene from ever asking him anything about his build or any other subject besides the mail, wings B and C, and the command offices. He clumsily unbuttoned his fly and displayed a penis long and shiny as a boa constrictor.

The postmaster's office was a composite of the various clichés of the American nightmare: a half-crazed fanatical Mormon with an oversized male member, a cotton-field Negro, and an ambitious kike.

Joseph was a happy trooper. He struck up a close friendship with Sergeant Saul Gantz, a sick man, and with Lieutenant Colonel Andrew Adams, a hero of the Pacific. Gantz was his age. A survivor of the Pusan Perimeter. Joseph and he shared so many things, starting with Brooklyn. Saul was from Williamsburg, the orthodox Jewish neighborhood of the borough. They had the same roots, knew the same landscapes, spoke the same language. They could have been cousins or brothers, and in fact they were like the reflection, by now ancient, of a broken mirror.

Joseph was in university when Saul was fighting in the second reconnaissance battalion and the war was fucking with his head. For three years he'd drifted for more or less extended periods in and out of hospitals and the police academy where he'd failed the officer exam twice. They never talked about the war because Joseph didn't know what it was like and Saul had no words for it, nor probably the desire.

They'd walk along the bank to the Brooklyn pier to watch the eddies swirling around the rusted orange ferries in the Narrows and watch the colorless, formless throng of workers crammed onto the decks during the daily rush-hour commute. And the myriad of lanterns and neon lights dancing on the icy, unfathomable waters of the tidal strait. They talked politics, wondered if the depression on McCarthy's forehead was the mark of a satanic horn in the making or of its ablation. Joseph talked about Gena, because servicemen always have to talk about the beauty who's supposed to be languishing at home waiting for the soldier's return, and Saul listened with an infinite patience that neither George Hammerstein nor Aaron Falk, nor even Gena herself, possessed.

It was Saul who introduced Joseph to Andrew Adams. Adams was a playboy undeterred by a prosthetic leg. On the contrary. The slight disjointed movement of the hips gave him a rolling gait that accentuated his natural languor and casual detachment. For him, too, it was a cushy position. A well-deserved one after having been repatriated, seven years before, from a Japanese prisoner camp in Java, his leg shortened up to the knee.

Andrew, who was from the Upper East Side, was the husband of Frances and the beaming father of identical twin girls, blond as the Valkyrie.

Joe and Andrew had nothing in common, not age, not roots, not landscapes, not language, and yet they shared a passion for politics, and a nostalgic veneration for great men, like Abraham Lincoln and Franklin Roosevelt. They were liberal Democrats, New Yorkers, and it didn't much matter that they were born on opposite sides of the river. They were this fucking city, they breathed this same incredible fucking city with the same nostrils, with the same love, with the same ambition.

Joe was promoted to the rank of sergeant two months before his demobilization and the father celebrated the event, as usual, in his own peculiar way. He could have ordered a cake from Rosenthal's or Kossar's, had a barbecue like the Baker-Stones, in the backyard of the grocery, but that was not in the spirit of Rapp's Grocery, any more than a glass of champagne would have been and, stranger still, than a nice fatty piece of maatjes herring washed down with Canadian vodka.

The celebrations began on Shabbat when he saw his father, who was called to the Torah to read the weekly portion, approach the bimah and say *gomel*, the blessing pronounced after someone has survived a life-threatening event. What danger had Nach'm Rappaport escaped? Slipping on the sawdust? Cutting himself on a stubborn can lid? A holdup by the Rubinstein gang? A drowning? Was he back from a long journey across the oceans? Had this man, who seldom ventured even as far as the Lower East Side on the other side of the river, flown over the Bermuda Triangle? No, he'd replied to the beadle, I'm thanking the Holy One, Blessed be He, for returning my son to me in one piece from the army. After the havdalah blessing over a candle, spices, and wine that marks the end of Shabbat,

Nach'm drew his son into the alley by the store where the Plymouth De Luxe with its red-lead-colored fender was parked under the tarpaulin.

Like a dignitary unveiling a commemorative plaque, he pulled back the tarpaulin to reveal an almost brand-new Chevrolet, it too De Luxe, emerald green with a gray roof and a red-lead-colored front right wing.

"Why are you doing all this, *tate*? Your pickup is on its last legs. You should've bought yourself a decent used car."

"My pickup is more than enough for the store's needs, Yossele my son. You're going to fly places. One day or another I'll sell the business. It's not doing so well anymore. Everyone's leaving, as you know, and the ones who aren't are running up tabs or they have no more teeth. And with its criminal gangs of Cossacks, the neighborhood, as you know, isn't so safe anymore. I arrived here when I was your age, in 1910. It was a great big city of Yids, now it's a city of deviants. Sodomites live among us. Even our shul and the community center are funded by a pimp, a *svodnik* from Moldavanka. Fly away, escape this small world, *mein liebe*."

The young Rappaport looked at his father, a tiny figure of a man, forthright and shriveled, not so old . . . yet so old.

The grocery was floundering, and Joseph hadn't noticed a thing. In a single generation, his father, this immigrant whose studies had been interrupted at the heder, had crossed the Atlantic and begotten a free, well-educated American. He'd fed, clothed, and raised the apple of his eye and left it to America to educate him. He'd worked his fingers to the bone so that his son would be a *mensch*, a *mensch* with a Chevrolet. He was letting him know that he could leave now, that his role as a father had, if not come to an end, at least entered a new phase, that of delight in seeing his vineyard bear the fruits of a life of labor, uprightness, and *tzniut*, as it says in the Psalms.

Like a relay baton, he handed him the car keys, which he'd decorated with a blue-and-white ribbon tied around a small parchment containing the traveler's prayer.

The car, American symbol of success, synonymous with freedom, was the vehicle of transmission because freedom is the ability to travel, to discover, to say to society, "I have the means of being a modern citizen. I'm participating in the technological grandeur that has never ceased from conquering new territories." From Yossele, to Joseph, to Joe, this was the patronymic metamorphosis sought by the father who'd already shortened his store's name. "Joe Rapp." It sounded right, it sounded American. But not all areas of modern life, of his son's Americanization, sat as well in Nach'm's mind as Joseph would have liked, in particular with regard to marriage.

Gena had never been introduced to her lover's family. Hard to tell whether she suffered from this state of affairs or was indifferent to it. Joe hid nothing from her. He told her about his parents, his life in Brighton Beach, a childhood on the brink of destitution, and all the while he, the prince of the family, never lacked a thing. Actually, on closer scrutiny, Gena must have resented it.

Kennedy's victory against Cabot Lodge marked her definitive return to Port Jefferson, whereas George Hammerstein was kept on as part of the young senator's team. This time, no doubt about Gena's resentment. She was revolted by the hypocrisy with which she'd been sidelined. She'd been granted a kiss from the hero, all the girls had been granted a kiss from the new senator, a handshake from the campaign manager, and Ciao, thanks for volunteering! The guys stayed on, the girls were sent packing unless they were doing secretarial work.

She was furious, and though Joe Rapp didn't really back her then, when he was appointed Adams's adjunct for Wagner's campaign, he introduced her into the small team tasked with taking on the Tammany Hall candidates.

The whole gang was living between the Village and Chelsea. Joe shared a place with Falk, Hammerstein with his young girlfriend, a nineteen-year-old pianist and singer named Blossom who dropped him a year later to embark on a career in France, and Gena moved in with Kathy, the sister of Frances, Andrew's ethereal wife and mother of the adorable twins, Marian and Robin—you don't make these things up!

We all have a picture in our minds of what young people from different backgrounds, with progressive ideas, intent on breaking with tradition, were doing in a neighborhood like Greenwich Village at the time. Simply read Ginsberg and the fatality he describes. Well, in this case, nothing could be farther from the truth! These young people, who dressed like bank managers, complete with ties, dark suits, and white shirts with pointed collars, who breathed politics and networks from the time they woke up until they went to bed, and who forged, at night, in their beds, in the impossible darkness of the gritty, noisy, neon city, a destiny studded with victories and crowned with glories, were not Kerouacs or Corsos or Burroughs. In fact, like their parents, they dreamed of climbing the social ladder and accumulation. Though they walked through the same gateway—the Washington Square Arch—the poets were consumed with fire; our heirs, with cupidity.

We find them in the same bars on Sixth and Seventh Avenues, and in the jazz clubs where Blossom drags them. The poets sit at their table, Wagner's campaign team at theirs. The same music rings in their ears, Thad Jones, Mary Lou Williams, they shake together to the same beat of Zutty Singleton's drums—the poets start from reality to describe the dream, while the ambitious want to build reality from a dream. They have common enemies—fear, McCarthy the rabid crusader from Bethesda, and indifference, and sometimes they share their fears and their truths in the same beds, like Aaron Falk who discovered his homosexuality in the arms of Allen Ginsberg. There was Tammany Hall, the HQ, Wagner's and Adams's speeches, reports, polls, Times Square, the *New York Times*, there was also sex, the heady lure of power, and the perks to come.

Frances Adams who, at thirty-one, was the oldest of the group, was also the only wife, the only mother, the only one to be "dutybound," to have signed a contract with the morality of White Anglo-Saxon Protestant institutions. Can we talk about Frances as being connected to the group? She was not in the Party, didn't participate in the discussions or libations in the smoke-filled bars of the Village. In fact, the young housewife, who was supposed to be responsible for the education and well-being of her twins, with Rosy, the live-in maid, actually abandoned their care to the young woman from Harlem. But who could expect an Upper East Side Madame Bovary to be enthusiastic about her status as mother, hostess, and ethereal beauty queen there to make her husband's prosthetic leg even more beautiful and heroic?

Joe Rapp rose quickly through the ranks of the new Mayor Wagner's office. In charge of the economic facets of the city's anti-discrimination project, he was the one to derail the promising political career of his friend and former roommate George Hammerstein, son of a Newark tanner. It was a tragic change of life for Hammerstein who already pictured himself, in five or six years, as attorney general of Manhattan, and who lost the same year the delightful madness of Blossom and the friendship of his classmate from university.

Back in the Garden State, he embarked on a career as a corporate lawyer, a junior partner in one of the top firms in Englewood. The day his father died, he tore up his Party card and all the letters and pictures of his faraway lover even as she announced her return to New York, under the wing of Norman Grantz who signed her to record on his Verve label. The following year, Hammerstein married a nice girl named Thelma, who was raising her ten-year-old daughter Tal on her own, and to whom he gave his name if not his attention.

Before long, the center of gravity of the young Democrat forces shifted north to the Upper East Side in Manhattan. Adams's sprawling apartment on 81st Street replaced the small bars in the Village. Frances wasn't exactly the ideal hostess for her husband Andrew, who was New York's Democratic hope, or would be, if only the senatorial seat that was clinging to former governor Herbert Lehman's ass could be detached from the impeccable pleats of his pants.

Andrew, who counted among the senator's official supporters since the first half of his term in office, had absolutely no choice but to betray his mentor during the

1953 primaries. Herbert Lehman was close to Eleanor and Mayor Wagner, the left wing of the Party, so challenging him meant securing the blessings of Tammany Hall, Carmine De Sapio, the crime boss Costello, and the Irish.

Frances Adams, in her stylish fuchsia cocktail dress, approached the corner of the living room where Joseph-Joe Rapp was brooding.

"Would you like a cup of coffee or a drink?"

Since he didn't reply, absorbed as he was in his post-adolescent gloom, she observed him for some time. She stood there peering at him as if she'd never peered at anyone before. She was trying to read under his skin. Behind his half-closed eyelids and the frown at the corners of his mouth, prematurely weary for his age.

"Would you like coffee, Joseph?" she repeated in a very low voice.

He raised his eyes, stared without seeing her, and, wholly sunk in his secret haze, cracked a smile so ironic that Frances could hear the malicious laugh that shook him inside.

"No, thanks," he got up abruptly as if propelled from the chair by an electric shock.

He left the Adams apartment without a word.

Joe Rapp joined the opposite side, the mayor's, and served him with loyalty, efficiency, and ferocity, virtues recompensed by an office at Gracie Mansion on the boss's floor. A big office with green shutters that he left closed at all hours in all seasons, turning his back on the sight of the maples in the park sloping down to the river and the finger of Roosevelt Island pointing to Astoria.

Aaron Falk, now gaunter and grayer, joined Joe's camp. The poet, his lover, had left, gone. The son of a bitch! Aaron didn't go to Frisco when Allen read *Howl*. Allen had not even given him a small entry ticket to his logorrhea: was he the unknown, one of the nameless beggars?

Holy Peter holy Allen holy Solomon holy Lucien holy Kerouac holy Huncke holy Burroughs holy Cassady holy the unknown buggered and suffering beggars holy the hideous human angels!

Dirty son of a bitch! Sucked, loved, smoked, imbibed, exposed and not a word, not one holy Aaron, holy Falk. Nada.

It was Officer Saul Gantz who broke the news to Joseph Rappaport of the death of their friend, Ezra Dickson University's best left-handed pitcher. Falk had been found unconscious in the squalid bathroom of a Harlem club, a syringe stuck in the left-handed pitcher's right arm.

Holy Falk, precise pitcher, vicious slider, pierced angel . . .

Conjuncture of circumstances—one can never be too negative about conjunctures of circumstances. *Tsushstandn* was the word that came to Nach'm Rappaport's mind to express his sense of powerlessness. Whenever something escaped his will or his comprehension, this pious Jew, who put his faith in the will of an all-powerful and righteous God, would avow that some "circumstances" were outside the divine plan and the logic of the world. *Tsushstandn* was not a pleasant word. There were no positive "conjunctures of circumstances" in Rappaport's language and world.

It was no doubt in the framework of these famous conjunctures of circumstances that, upon leaving the cemetery where Falk's burial had just ended, Joe Rapp heard Frances's slightly nasal, husky voice behind his back.

"Joseph, could you take me back to my place?"

A few moments before, their eyes had met at the graveyard while he read, in a shrill, mechanical voice, the short tribute he'd written that very morning in his office.

" . . . The best left-handed pitcher—no Warren Spahn, to be sure, but the most powerful pitcher on the mound at Ezra Dickson University."

Frances's husband Andrew hadn't shown up, probably because of Joe and his "betrayal." It was a colder than usual late-winter day. Between the graves, the dirt-crusted snow looked like black crystal. Hammerstein was there with his wife Thelma, averting her eyes from the speaker's gaze, staring at her pumps splashing in the sodden grass.

Gena too had come, had gratified him with a dry peck. He didn't know how she'd heard about Aaron. From the

NYT? Surely not, at any rate, from the obituary section of the Yiddish paper, the *Forward*. Gena Baker-Stone, the shikse from Port Jefferson, looked pinker and fresher than a little C-cup piglet. She didn't stay to watch the burial ceremony. Gena didn't see Aaron's father tear the fabric of his shirt at the collar or his mother, eyes closed, put a white stone on the little mound of earth just raised by the scruffy bearded men from the *Hevre Kadishe*, a mound for Ezra Dickson's best left-handed pitcher.

When he turned to Frances to answer her, he confusedly sensed that the paternal *Tsushstandn* would be sitting behind them on the rear seat of his brand-new Chrysler Saratoga.

She took him in her mouth, and he let her. He watched her blond hair scatter over his lap, ravel around the gearshift, unravel over the pinstripes of his pants, fan out into light. The dark pheromonal web swaddled them, kept them warm, in the steamy interior of the Chrysler Saratoga.

Covert passions in hotel rooms, motel hookups, fortuitous encounters. Kisses, tears, caresses, lust, flowing juices, exchanged, consumed, licked. Joseph was intoxicated by this ideal sex that involved nothing but his vital energy and appetite. Frances, the unfaithful wife, dreamed of fidelity, eternity, sanctity—in short, of divorce, marriage, a recomposed family, a big house in the Hamptons, a dog on the lawn, and, why not, a proud American flag billowing in the ocean wind.

These are the circumstances that escaped the grasp of their victims. The web appeared suddenly, shiny as coal, slimy as a black snake from Mexico, when Joseph-Joe Rappaport gave Frances the news that he was going to marry Jill Halpern, the daughter of Randall J. Halpern of Halpern & Cortland Inc. from Duluth, Minnesota.

What did she expect from him? That he would remain her lover? The eternal cock? Damn it! He had a father, a career, a fucking religion that said that a good yid marries a good yid under a fucking wedding canopy and not a passionate, melancholic shikse. What did she expect from him?

He'd arrived at this point in his thoughts, in his anger too, when his old buddy Saul Gantz, now a police sergeant, asked to meet up in a Lower East Side coffee shop—sticky Formica table and overpowering smell of cinnamon. Saul was already seated; the owner was pouring steaming coffee into his cup. He'd lost weight again, but his features seemed less marked, less legible, more detached no doubt. He was fiddling around with a rugelach, crushed to a pulp in the center of a saucer.

"Last night the Adams came as a couple to the station," he paused. "They didn't want to see me 'cause they know we're friends, so they went to Lieutenant . . . "

Joe listened without understanding what it was about, but his body clearly felt the birth of something like a tumor, a tremendous threat.

"Joseph, they filed charges against you," he paused again, "for attempted rape."

The following day, the *Post*, on page 3, featured a short piece with all the ingredients of an ugly scandal involving sex, violence, and politics.

RAPE: POLICE OPEN INVESTIGATION INTO A CLOSE ADVISOR TO THE MAYOR

The wife of a prominent young political figure in the local Democratic Party, a hero from the war in the Pacific, filed charges in the Upper East Side police station against an important advisor in Gracie Mansion, a friend of the couple and former collaborator of the plaintiff. The Manhattan District Attorney has opened a criminal investigation.

On his desk, the green opaline lamp, positioned perpendicular to the photo of the home run, illuminated the newspaper opened to page 3. The spectacular dive at Stuyvesant High School caught by the photograph in the *Brooklyn Herald* no longer held the glare of the lamp. In the shadows, it was nothing more than a dive, a haphazard foot flung onto a 17-by-8.5-by-12-inch pentagonal plate, a disequilibrium, a fall.

IT WAS GOING TO BE MY LAST BEER

To R. Carver

Vlad slammed it down in front of me, the glass dripping over with frothy foam. He grumbles that I have five minutes to drink up and get out. And to emphasize his point, he exaggerates his tired club-footed gait, scraping the grimy bar floor.

"Damn it, Ray! Been at it for fifteen hours, so chop-chop, drink up, and let me get back to my crib."

Vlad tosses the now stale leftover coffee into the sink, and I toss a dime into the jukebox mounted on the wall near the counter. The light turns blue when the coin drops with a brief metallic clink. The articulated arm begins its circle dance on the vinyl disk. I sip my beer listening to Carmen McRae while Vlad refills the napkin dispensers, muttering nasty expletives in Polish or Ukrainian.

A couple that was lingering on a threadbare banquette in the rear decides to leave. She can't be more than eighteen.

The guy looks like an accountant and is wearing an accountant's synthetic suit. He helps the kid into her pink rabbit-skin coat. When they push the door open, a gust of damp, snow-laden air rushes into the bar.

I put a dollar on the countertop, still damp from Vlad's sponge, and walk out on the last note of "My Foolish Heart."

. The girl is alone, her forehead on the steering wheel of an old Ford. Her car and mine are the only ones left in the parking lot and snow feathers begin to fall. The neon Diner & Bar sign goes out, then the Budweiser logo.

The road is straight and dark.

It'll take at least two hours before I get to the lake and the night will still be dark and deep.

The snow has stopped falling. The road winding its way through the forest of larches and firs turns pitch black. I hum "My Foolish Heart."

Since leaving Vlad's bar, I haven't seen red taillights heading to the lake or yellow headlights heading back to the city. The only lights were, less than an hour ago, from the pupils of a stag staring stunned in the middle of the road. My heart is still reverberating like Max Roach's drums. I don't know if it's the abruptness, the sudden braking, or the utter beauty of the sight. There he was with the antlers of a young buck. His flanks swelled from his vaporous breathing. Firmly planted on his already solid legs, he stared at me without stirring apart from the involuntary movement of his breathing, a sort of elegance of his petrified life.

I turned off my lights, but he stayed where he was. He was staring at me. I could sense his presence now more than I could see him. I even had time to light a cigarette. It must have been the flame of my Zippo that finally convinced him that he had legs and that his place wasn't in the middle of the road, even if this chaotic strip of cracked asphalt led to the lake and nowhere else.

At the Welcome to Greene County sign, the road twisted and turned for a good half an hour. The damn deer had been luckier than the deer that had cut across our path. Joan and I. That was more than twenty years ago!

As I sank back into the past, I couldn't help glancing in the rearview mirror, a reflex perhaps to blunt the leap of memory and especially its impact.

The deer hadn't been as lucky back then. I was too stoned and he too dumb to understand that my old Oldsmobile and the snow were about to hatch a plot against nature. Joan had cried as I wrapped his body, throbbing and smeared with blood, in an old plaid blanket that my father always left on the rear seat.

The Catskill Sheriff's assistant had emptied the trunk, laughing, and his gun into the deer's head, still laughing. Joan had cried.

On the side of a bridge, my headlights shine on a faded poster announcing Jerry Lewis for July 4, 1963, at Kutsher's Hotel.

The lake is there, and I don't see it. It's hiding, in the fog that protects it, like an animal ready to pounce. I can sense it, just as a few minutes before I'd smelled Joan's perfume.

HAMLET TO QUEENS

July 17, 1967

On the drive up the coast, I'd been tempted at least ten times to stop at one of the many lobster-roll shacks by the gas stations. The more or less elaborate signs boasted, sometimes with neon lights, the best rolls in the county. Hunger had been nagging me since Jacksonville and since I'm the Pavlovian drooler type of guy, saliva was dribbling from my mouth like some fuckin' bulldog.

I hit it on the nail. A parking lot facing the ocean. A dozen tables covered with filthy oilcloth and a redhead pin-up, pouting, busty and ten feet tall, awaiting your order.

As the sun always rises to the east, I had the show-off right in my face and had to look for shade behind the apron of the pin-up which had undergone a great many graphic and anatomical abuses over time.

The station attendant, a young yokel in overalls, served me the roll in a cardboard sleeve with an ice-cold can of

7 Up dripping with sweat. Expertly he tossed a napkin dispenser to the center of the table and, as he turned on his heels back to the prefab, he gestured with an authoritative finger to the metal garbage can that stood prominently on the boundary between the parking area and the "terrace."

The tide was low and revealed sandbars teeming with living organisms. What God could possibly have been thinking when he created them was beyond me, unless it was to feed the lobsters of Cape Lookout.

The specialty hereabouts is doused in lemon juice, slathered in hot butter, and served on a soft hot-dog bun studded with toasted sesame seeds. It wasn't bad at all and, as I was about to get up to order another roll, this time with mayonnaise, like it's served between New York and Boston, a big red-and-white Chevy pickup pulled up and parked a few inches from the driver side of my car, clearly obstructing access to my door.

A girl and two boys who barely filled out their jeans, jerseys, and felt hats spilled out of the pickup and headed, as I did, to the gas station and the prefab. Scraggly teenagers at loose ends. The attendant in blue overalls sent them packing.

"No beer yesterday, no beer today or tomorrow, and that's the way it'll be kiddoes 'til your fuckin' birthday."

They kept at him for a while without pushing his hot temper over the edge.

Once served, I headed back to my table whose linoleum top was beginning to warp in the sun. The kids were hanging around their pickup. I motioned to the girl who seemed on the whole to have more syntax than the others.

"There are some cans left over from a pack in my trunk—help yourselves, they won't be ice cold, but at least they'll taste like beer."

They sat down at my table and in return for the beers they dangled a joint so huge under my nose that no young man with any common sense would have turned it down.

They asked me where I came from, where I was going, what I was doing in the area, who I was, and that sort of thing.

I told them I was Alex from Newark, that I worked for a New York music magazine, and that I was driving back from Hamlet to my new digs in Queens.

They told me about a whole bunch of local singers whom I'd never heard of and poked fun at me as they guzzled and burped my last six beers.

I was sweating when I decided to hit the road before the second joint they were rolling would be passed around and leave me wasted on oilcloth stinking from the tide.

They didn't budge, merely saw me off with a friendly gesture of clinking cans. To get into my old Ford, I had to climb over the passenger seat. I splashed my face with a little water. Soda, weed, lobster, and mayonnaise, all came back up to the edges of my lips. I opened the window wide, turned on the radio to a national station to avoid having to hear country music. It must have been three in the afternoon when the news presenter announced John Coltrane's death last night in New York. The urge to puke was stronger than anything. I chucked two Cape Lockout lobster rolls onto the pickup of my new friends.

They walked over chuckling.

The girl, who must have been barely sixteen and had a stork bite that marred half her cheek, pulled a rifle from a satchel attached to the pickup bed.

"Around here, we don't like kikes who puke our lobsters and cry about niggers."

She was the one who fired the shot, I'm sure of it, and they all laughed.

A LUNCH OF LIGHT

A LUNCH OF LIGHT—I

Ten years ago still, she was long and slender, her skin responsive and fair, her movements lively, her eyes bright, only ten years ago.

Goldie has ceased suffering, he thought, his ear pressed to her chest. The nightgown, like a tea bag, held the dry effluence. Like a tea bag, it had absorbed all of Max's tears.

When things went badly in them, around them, in spite of them, because of them, Max and Goldie made the peace of bodies, then of souls numbed by sleep, then of awakenings bathed in the sunlight of Edenic truths, of the very first morning.

Five years ago already, the powerful light that emanated from her began dimming little by little. Bulb after bulb. Silently they despaired of relighting them.

It was a superhuman effort. Just as a kiss came to restore the weakened filaments, a new shadow would appear somewhere else. Under her chest, under her throat, under her lips, under her sunken belly. Goldie was disappearing into the transparency of a skin that revealed her patience as much as her suffering. Max slept by her side. Their arms were entwined. He slept and she, she watched over him as she'd always done. For so long already, at night, he dreamed dreams she no longer dreamed, and, in daytime, she took upon herself the nightmares she wanted to spare him.

A few days ago still, Max had seen, in the half-light of the bedroom, Goldie's soul somewhere deep down in her chest. It was there, bright and dazzling, joyful, divine, proud, free, and reassuring. He'd fallen asleep in the crook of her armpit, inhaling, like a diver before the apnea, the last gulp of air, Goldie's living essences. And by the sacrifice of his breathing, filling his beloved with the life that was escaping from between her lips in a hot, sour mist.

A few hours ago still, Goldie had grasped his hand, and her hand, shriveled and pale, was like a vine in winter before pruning, bristling with shoots reaching with love for the sky.

A few minutes ago still, Goldie had parted, withdrawn from her gentle presence to the world of eyes, mouth, and voice. In the dappled half-light of the summer stars, Max had seen everything within her gathering within him.

Now, Max was eating Goldie's body. Crushing it between his jaws, welcoming into his viscera his wife's viscera and her diaphanous flesh.

He was making for himself a joyful funeral, a human burial, a sensual sepulcher, the last receptacle of this interminable love.

Now they were two in one, he was They, she and he, masculine feminine, the Edenic dream like the very first morning.

A LUNCH OF LIGHT — II

The bone was white. "Radiant," Max heard himself say. And then softly sang "radiant Goldie, white and sublime . . . my sweet sunshine." His voice was charming for his age.

Yesterday, he'd feasted on a grilled shoulder seasoned with garlic and rosemary. This evening he was having Florentine-style tripes and tomorrow will be tomorrow and he'll still be hungry. Maybe some morels from this sweet season of rebirth. Maybe some crème fraîche and charred peppercorns like in that restaurant on Place de la Bourse in Brussels where Goldie and he had surrendered for the first time to the forbidden delights of hidden caresses.

The bone was white, the flesh had come off the bone and it appeared white. The meat had shredded into filaments and fibers, the fats had dissolved, forming rillettes.

Since Goldie's death, Max had sat at the table, attached to his inexorable sepulchral destiny.

The first to go had made the survivor promise and the survivor had promised the first to go.

In this way, final *Hevre Kadishe*, he buried his beloved's body in his loving body and the beloved thus mingled for a moment with the visceral soul of the lover.

For the time of digestion.

A LUNCH OF LIGHT—III

When Lieutenant Saul Gantz of the NYPD stepped into the apartment, he contained an unmistakable urge to puke the hot-dog-sauerkraut-fried-onions-horseradish combo that he'd just wolfed down, elbows on the metal counter of Marcus's truck.

The old-fashioned apartment was well kempt. The hardwood floor was newly waxed, and everything was tidy and dusted. The antimacassars on the two green suede armchairs were an immaculate starch-gleaming white.

On the faux-marble countertop in the kitchen, a blue porcelain teapot and the red label of a bergamot tea bag dangling from its side. Not a crumb on the oilcloth table covering and, on the sideboard, a pile of clean plates with gold edging. Yet, the apartment on St. Marks Place had the stench of a butcher's backroom in the Meatpacking District during a heat wave. A nauseating, metallic, mucky, terrifying smell.

The coroner was having the body of an old man removed. The stretcher seemed light. Uncannily light, as if the two attendants were walking out with nothing on it. On the bed in the apartment's only bedroom, barely an impression from the body on the fluffy duvet.

The coroner, before leaving, diagnosed death by poisoning. The empty bottle of barbiturates, next to an empty stemmed glass, bore out his conclusion.

But you don't send a homicide lieutenant to the scene of a suicide on a 98-degree Sunday in the month of August. You do send a homicide lieutenant to the scene though, even on a Sunday in August, even when the sun is melting the asphalt on Broadway, when the policemen, called to the dead man's domicile because of the smell, have discovered human remains, admittedly few, in the vegetable bin and icebox of the fridge.

Opening the windows had provided little relief, only adding to the stomach-churning rotting meat, the stink rising from the garbage cans in the courtyard.

Dusk was falling little by little, creeping over the roofs and the overheated railings of fire escapes and rusty ladders. Lieutenant Gantz sat on one of the two armchairs opposite the massive TV set with its curved screen encased in a faux-walnut frame.

The last man from forensics had left long ago. The open front door was barred by a yellow ribbon marked "crime scene." The lieutenant had searched the apartment meticulously, drawer by drawer, buffet, dresser, wardrobe. He had slowly leafed through Max and Goldie's photo albums. The prints, yellowed with age, showed the faces of anonymous bearded old men and pudgy children. Some in Bessarabia villages, others on the beach in Coney Island or in front of a bungalow in the Catskills.

He eventually found a handwritten letter in a large, slanted script that began with these words:

My dear children,

I will soon be leaving this wonderful world of joy and now of suffering. I've loved you all my life. You have been for us the miraculous gift of our love.

But you know all this, as you have witnessed our mad, immense passion.

By the time you read these words, I'll be gone and your father who's holding my hand will join me on this leg of our journey. We are afraid of this unknown destination and dread traveling there alone.

It's madness, I confess, but your father and I have reached a deep agreement not to outlive each other and to serve as the sepulcher to the first to go, so that we will be one body for all eternity . . .

Saul Gantz dropped the letter on his lap and shut his eyes.

Later when the night had plunged the walls and knick-knacks into darkness, he'd taken a deep breath of the perfume from a bottle neatly placed on a small glass table in the bathroom and beheld suddenly, in the distressed mirror, the frail silhouettes of an old woman and an old man walking into the distance with the same steady step, hand in hand.

GLOSSARY

Hevre Kadishe: Literally "Holy Society," this is an organization of Jewish men and women who see to it that the bodies of deceased Jews are prepared for burial according to Jewish tradition and are protected from desecration until burial.

Shaharit: Morning prayer services.

tzniut: Humility, modesty, and discretion.

Tammany Hall: Political organization that was the political engine of the Democratic Party in New York for more than 170 years and contributed to the election of mayors, prosecutors, and judges.

yiddische tate: Jewish father.